D1369563

Jim Henson's™

SPLASH AND BUBBLES™

Rhythm of the Reef

Based on the series created by John Tartaglia
Based on the TV series teleplay written by Mark Drop
Adaptation by Liza Charlesworth

Houghton Mifflin Harcourt
Boston   New York

ISBN: 978-1-328-85277-9 paper over board
ISBN: 978-1-328-85278-6 paperback

hmhco.com

Printed in China
SCP 10 9 8 7 6 5 4 3 2 1
4500695641

Splash was excited! It was the day of the Reeftown Rhythm Festival.

He swam over to see if his pal Wave was ready to go.

"Today's the big day!" said Splash.

But the friendly octopus didn't budge.

"You go ahead and have yourself a boppin' good time," said Wave.

"Oh, I will! See you there, Wave," he said.
Then off he swam.

FIN FACT:
There are more than
100 different kinds of octopuses.
The smallest is the size of a dime
and the biggest is as wide as a
house from tentacle tip to
tentacle tip. Wow!

Wave sighed. He wanted to go to the festival too. But he was afraid—afraid to dance.

Splash stopped to pick up his other pals on the way.
Bubbles couldn't wait to show off her fancy dance moves.
"Let's go shake a tail fin!" she giggled.

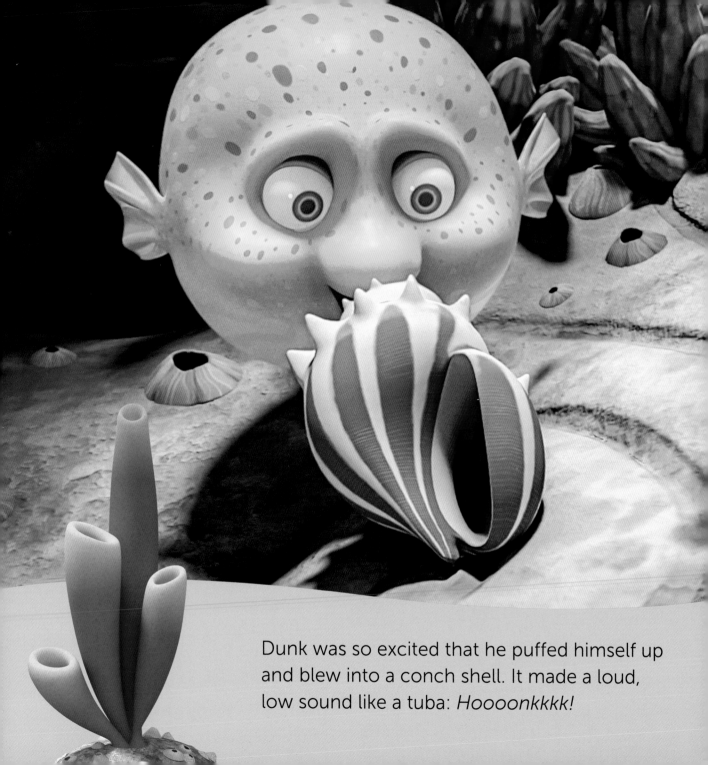

Dunk was so excited that he puffed himself up and blew into a conch shell. It made a loud, low sound like a tuba: *Hoooonkkkk!*

The noise was so loud that it woke up Ripple's whole family!

"Shhh! I think a couple hundred of my brothers were still sleeping," she said.

Dunk apologized. Then away they all swam to the big event.

At last the friends arrived at Coral Cove. The music sounded so *fintastic* that they couldn't help but bob along.

The reef was really rocking! Mayor Sting swayed by, Denny the cleaner shrimp waved her antennae, and even Zee did a shark shimmy. But Wave was nowhere to be found.

FIN FACT:
Octopuses are invertebrates—they don't have bones. So they can squeeze into small spaces to hide. What *do* octopuses have? Eight tentacles covered with suction cups. If they lose a tentacle, it will grow back!

Wave was still at Take-Off Point.

"How come you're not down at the festival shaking a tentacle?" Splash asked.

"I really shouldn't dance on account of my fragile bones," Wave explained.

"Ha-ha!" said Splash. "I happen to know that octopuses don't have *any* bones!"

"The truth is, I can't dance," Wave said sadly. To prove it, he showed off his moves. He wiggled. He waggled. He wobbled.

"I think your dancing is *fantastic!*" Splash said. He liked his friend *and* his wild moves.

That made Wave feel good—so good that he decided to go to the festival after all.

Meanwhile, the kids were having a blast. Boy, did they boogie!
"So have you heard about Dunk's new dance?" Maury asked.
"It's all anyone is talking about!"

Dunk swelled bigger and bigger until he nearly popped. What was the name of that cool move? "I call it 'The Puffer,'" he said proudly.

At last Splash returned to the festival. And he had Wave with him.

"Wave, you came to the party!" said Dunk.

"He did more than come to the party. He brought the moves!" said Splash. "Check it out!"

Wave wiggled. He waggled. He wobbled. After a while, Wave was feeling pretty good about his dancing skills.

But Flo thought Wave's moves meant he was in trouble. She swam right over.

"It's okay, everyone," she said. "Wave just needs a little help! He's lost control of his tentacles!"

Wave felt embarrassed. "I was just dancing," he said.

"Oh, I'm sorry!" said Flo. She swam away.

"I knew I had no place at any rhythm festival," Wave said sadly.

"The important thing is that you're here with your friends and you're having fun," Splash said.

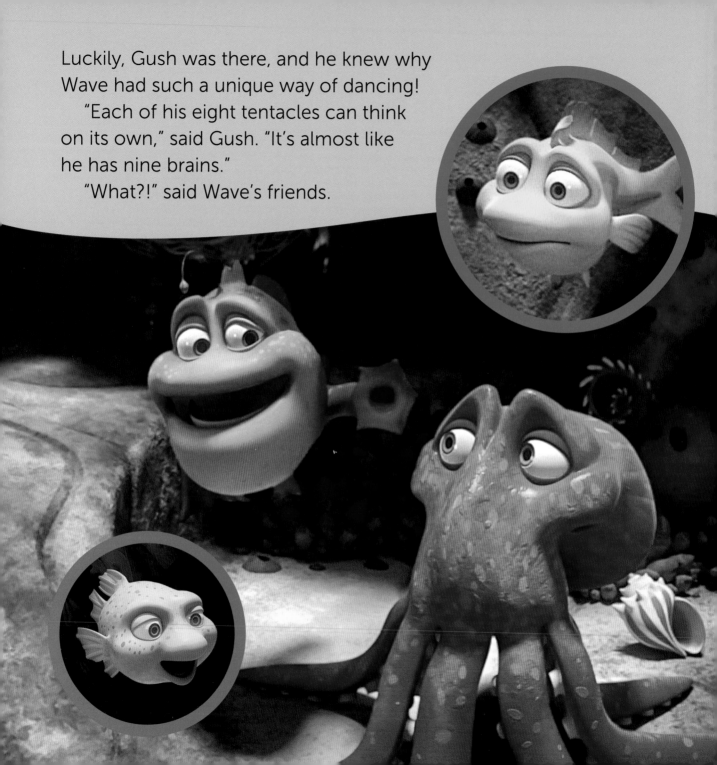

Luckily, Gush was there, and he knew why Wave had such a unique way of dancing!

"Each of his eight tentacles can think on its own," said Gush. "It's almost like he has nine brains."

"What?!" said Wave's friends.

FIN FACT:
An octopus has a mass of neurons inside each tentacle, as well as in its head. The brain can send each one a different message, so each tentacle "thinks" on its own. This is how octopuses can do many different things at once!

"Wow!" cried Bubbles. "That must be why some consider the octopus the smartest invertebrate in the sea."

"The smartest invertebrate in the sea!" Wave said. That made him feel so wonderful that he began to dance again. Wiggle. Waggle. Wobble.